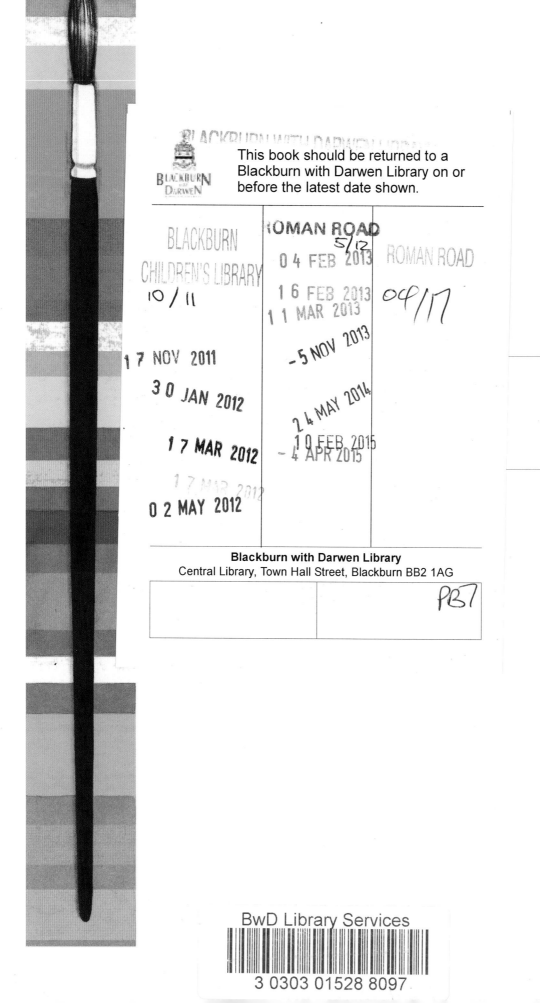

For Brian and Mathew

First published in Great Britain in 2011 by
Gullane Children's Books
185 Fleet Street, London, EC4A 2HS
www.gullanebooks.com

10 9 8 7 6 5 4 3 2 1

Text and illustrations © Sarah Massini 2011

hb ISBN: 978-1-86233-804-3
pb ISBN: 978-1-86233-820-3

Printed and bound in China.

If I Could Paint the World

Sarah Massini

GULLANE
CHILDREN'S BOOKS

If I could paint the world,
I wonder what colour it would be.

Would the grass be green?

Would the sun be yellow?

Would the sky be blue?

I wonder.

I think
I'll paint
everything...

PINK!

Pink sun.

Pink grass.

Pink sky.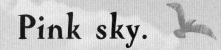

My brother
just **loves** it!

"Pink stinks!"

For breakfast, I'll paint
red juice, and **purple cornflakes** with **orange milk.**

And for my brother?
Green muffin
and green **butter.**

"delicious!
Thanks!"

CRUNCHY
CRISP
CORNFLAK

"You're welcome!"

We'll both brush our teeth . . .

with **black toothpaste!**

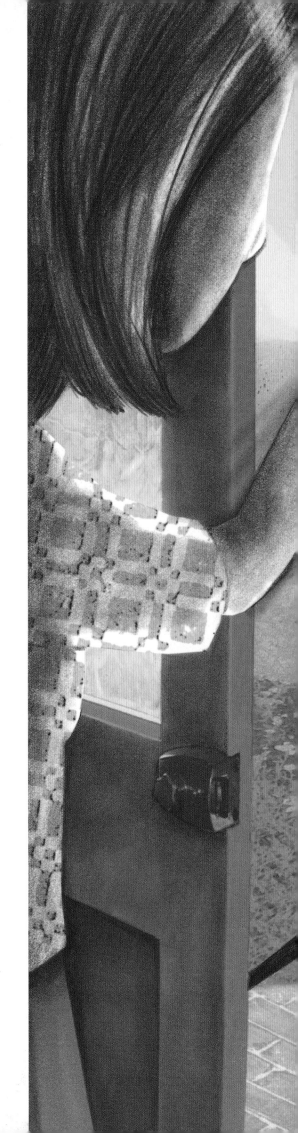

Then the school bus arrives, just like any other morning. Well, almost...

Today everything's going to be **orange**.

"Bye, Mum!"

Wait,
purple is better.

Or ... **red!**

"That'll do," says Miss Brightly.
"Now let's have a story."

Hmm...

I think I'll make some changes.
Meet **Little Lilac
Riding Hood** ...

"Hee hee! grandma won't recognise me!"

and **Pea Green**
and her seven dwarves!

"who is the greenest of us all?"

By Appointment to
Her Majesty Ye
WICKED QUEEN

Ye All-Over
GREENING
LOTION

It's time for my favourite lesson – art!
We're copying a famous painting...

in our own special way!

"WOW!"

"If you can paint the world," says my brother, "then I want a red racing car!"

"Yes, and we want big blue bugs...

a peppermint puppy...

a purple pig...

a pink panda..."

I say,
"That'll do."

But then everyone joins in.

"Let's have orange kites!"

"And lilac lights!"

"Green hearts!"

"And yellow tarts!"

I wonder.

If **you** could paint *your* world,
what colour would it be?

Would it be pink
    or orange
        or purple?

It's probably just as well,
when you **think** about it . . .

that the grass is **green,**

the sun is **yellow**

and the sky is (mostly) **blue.**

Because when you *really* think about it, the world is perfect...

exactly as it is.

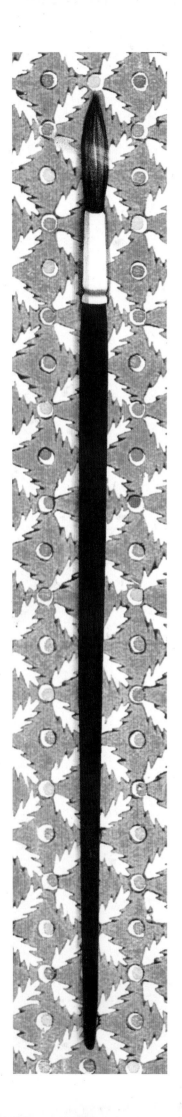

Other books for you to enjoy...

Doodleday
Ross Collins

Mum has just one thing to tell Harvey on Doodleday – no drawing allowed. But surely one little fly won't hurt? Not until Harvey's fly comes to life and starts to wreck the kitchen, that is! Soon all Harvey's doodles are rampaging out of control – and only one person is capable of stopping them . . .

Immi
Karin Littlewood

One day Immi finds a colourful wooden bird at the end of her fishing line. Day after day, more beautiful objects appear, and visitors soon flock to Immi's white world. But where do these bright gifts come from? And how can she thank her unknown friend for the joy they have given her?

Mimi Make-Believe
Claire Freedman
illustrated by Gemma Raynor

Pirates! Explorers! Cowboys! Mimi loves to make believe . . . but as for making friends, she's far too shy. Until one day she hears a "HELP! HELP!" coming from next door. Can Mimi summon her courage and jump to the rescue?!

Billy Bean's Dream
Simone Lia

Billy Bean doesn't expect his dream of building a rocket to ever get off the ground. But when two yellow jelly beans find his rocket plan and arrive with useful tools and plenty of friends to help, it looks like Billy's fantasy may come true after all!